GOLD
STANDARD

Cherry Tree Elementary
Media Center
Carmel, IN 46033

WORDS THAT SHAPED AMERICA

THE MOST POWERFUL WORDS ABOUT CIVIL RIGHTS

I HAVE A DREAM

BY SARAH SMYKOWSKI

Gareth Stevens
PUBLISHING

Please visit our website, www.garethstevens.com. For a free color catalog of all our high-quality books, call toll free 1-800-542-2595 or fax 1-877-542-2596.

Library of Congress Cataloging-in-Publication Data
Names: Smykowski, Sarah, author.
Title: The most powerful words about civil rights / Sarah Smykowski.
Description: New York : Gareth Stevens Publishing, 2020. | Series: Words
   that shaped America | Includes index.
Identifiers: LCCN 2019026605 | ISBN 9781538248003 | ISBN 9781538248010
   (library binding) | ISBN 9781538247990 (paperback) | ISBN 9781538248027
   (ebook)
Subjects: LCSH: African Americans--Civil rights--History--20th
   century--Juvenile literature. | Civil rights movements--United
   States--History--20th century--Juvenile literature. | African
   Americans--Civil rights--History--20th century--Quotations. | Civil
   rights movements--United States--History--20th century--Quotations.
Classification: LCC E185.61 .S6574 2020 | DDC 323.1196/073--dc23
LC record available at https://lccn.loc.gov/2019026605

First Edition

Published in 2020 by
Gareth Stevens Publishing
111 East 14th Street, Suite 349
New York, NY 10003

Copyright © 2020 Gareth Stevens Publishing

Designer: Sarah Liddell
Editor: Therese Shea

Photo credits: Cover, p. 1 (main) OttawaAC/Wikimedia Commons; cover, p. 1 (inset) ProhibitOnions/Wikimedia Commons; ink smear used throughout Itsmesimon/ Shutterstock.com; border used throughout igorrita/Shutterstock.com; background used throughout Lukasz Szwaj/Shutterstock.com; p. 4 Parhamr/Wikimedia Commons; p. 5 Rena Schild/Shutterstock.com; p. 7 A Fellow Editor/Wikimedia Commons; pp. 8, 9, 17 (top), 18, 21, 23 (lunch counter sit-in) Bettmann/Contributor/Bettmann/Getty Images; p. 10 Donaldson Collection/Contributor/Michael Ochs Archives/Getty Images; p. 11 (flyer) photo courtesy of Library of Congress; p. 11 (Montgomery Bus Boycott) Don Cravens/Contributor/The LIFE Images Collection/Getty Images; p. 13 (mug shot) Akerlea Velázquez/Wikimedia Commons; p. 13 (photo) P. S. Burton/Wikimedia Commons; p. 15 (MLK) Francis Miller/Contributor/ The LIFE Picture Collection/Getty Images; p. 15 (March on Washington) Paul Schutzer/ Contributor/ The LIFE Picture Collection/Getty Images; p. 17 (bottom) Emijrp/Wikimedia Commons; p. 19 Davepape/Wikimedia Commons; pp. 20, 27 (Shirley Chisholm) Adam Cuerden/ Wikimedia Commons; p. 23 (Diane Nash) Afro Newspaper/Gado/Contributor/Archive Photos/Getty Images; p. 24 Tom/Wikimedia Commons; p. 27 (Dorothy Height) Fæ/Wikimedia Commons.

All rights reserved. No part of this book may be reproduced in any form without permission in writing from the publisher, except by a reviewer.

Printed in the United States of America

Some of the images in this book illustrate individuals who are models. The depictions do not imply actual situations or events.

CPSIA compliance information: Batch #CW20GS; For further information contact Gareth Stevens, New York, New York at 1-800-542-2595.

CONTENTS

Words in the glossary appear in **bold** type
the first time they are used in the text.

A POWERFUL TOOL

"We hold these truths to be self-evident, that all men are created equal." Long ago, these words from the Declaration of Independence defined an event: the founding of a new nation, the United States of America. Nearly two centuries later, Americans used these words as a powerful tool for change during the fight for civil rights in the 1950s and 1960s. Leaders and citizens called for all to share in the freedom and equality the Founding Fathers promised so many years before.

Whether spoken at rallies before millions of people, broadcast into homes through the TV or radio, or spread through song, certain words from the civil rights movement inspired a generation of Americans to fight for change. These words shaped America, and they continue to echo through history.

WHAT'S IN A WORD?

There's a famous saying: "The pen is mightier than the sword." It means that words have more power than violence. It also means that the impact of words lasts longer than the impact of fighting. There are many times throughout history where this has proven true, especially during the civil rights movement. Many **ACTIVISTS** felt nonviolence was the best way to fight and used their powerful words as weapons in the struggle for change.

STUDENTS GATHERED IN WASHINGTON, DC, IN 2013 TO HONOR THE 50TH ANNIVERSARY OF THE FAMOUS MARCH ON WASHINGTON, A DEFINING MOMENT IN THE CIVIL RIGHTS MOVEMENT.

BEHIND THE WORDS

CIVIL RIGHTS ARE PERSONAL RIGHTS GUARANTEED BY THE US CONSTITUTION AND FEDERAL LAWS. THEY INCLUDE THE RIGHT TO VOTE, THE RIGHT TO A FAIR TRIAL, AND THE RIGHT TO A PUBLIC EDUCATION.

ABOUT THE
MOVEMENT

Even though slavery had been made illegal officially in 1865, African American citizens continued to face inequality in society, especially in the South. This discrimination, or unequal treatment, meant African Americans often had to use separate public facilities and attend separate schools. They were even denied the right to vote. Though discriminatory, these practices were made legal through local and state laws.

BEHIND THE WORDS

THE 1896 US SUPREME COURT CASE, *PLESSY V. FERGUSON*, LEGALIZED "SEPARATE BUT EQUAL" PUBLIC FACILITIES. THIS PHRASE JUSTIFIED UNFAIR PRACTICES FOR DECADES.

The civil rights movement in the United States was an effort to end segregation and unequal treatment of African Americans under the law. During this time, activists and everyday citizens worked to gain equal rights for African Americans. Beginning in the 1950s, many people emerged as leaders of this movement, thanks to their brave acts and powerful words.

WHILE THE CIVIL RIGHTS MOVEMENT REACHED ITS HEIGHT IN THE 1950s AND 1960s, MUCH ACTIVISM OCCURRED BEFORE AND AFTER THIS PERIOD.

A HISTORIC STRUGGLE

While the founding documents of the United States promise liberty and equality for all men, history shows that this guarantee wasn't actually for everyone, or even for all men. Life for many African Americans was guided by laws that legalized segregation and racist practices that made them feel less than human. By the 1950s, black citizens rallied in large numbers to fight back against this unequal treatment. Activism entered courtrooms, schools, buses, workplaces, and everywhere in between.

NO PLACE FOR SEGREGATION

Some civil rights leaders sought to change society by changing the laws. One major challenge to segregation was the Supreme Court case *Brown v. Board of Education of Topeka*, which was actually a number of cases.

In the 1950s, several African American families filed lawsuits against school districts. In the case involving 8-year-old Linda Brown, her parents wanted her to attend the school closest to their home, which was only for whites. In other cases under *Brown v. Board of Education*, the issue was the poor quality of the schools for black children. The lawyers arguing for the African American families proved that segregation had terrible effects on black children. The Supreme Court decided, "In the field of public education . . . 'separate but equal' has no place. Separate educational facilities are **inherently** unequal."

THE NAACP

THE LAWYERS REPRESENTING THE PARENTS IN *BROWN V. BOARD OF EDUCATION*—INCLUDING FUTURE SUPREME COURT JUSTICE THURGOOD MARSHALL—WERE MEMBERS OF THE NATIONAL ASSOCIATION OF THE ADVANCEMENT OF COLORED PEOPLE (NAACP). FOUNDED IN 1909, THE NAACP WAS FORMED TO HELP AFRICAN AMERICANS GAIN THE RIGHTS THEY WERE PROMISED UNDER THE CONSTITUTION. MANY IMPORTANT CIVIL RIGHTS LEADERS WERE MEMBERS OF THE NAACP, INCLUDING W. E. B. DU BOIS AND MEDGAR EVERS. THE NAACP CONTINUES TO WORK AGAINST **PREJUDICE**, RACISM, AND DISCRIMINATION TODAY.

THE SUPREME COURT ORDERED THAT WHITES-ONLY PUBLIC SCHOOLS BE INTEGRATED, OR OPENED TO ALL. IT WOULD TAKE TIME—AND SOMETIMES THE ASSISTANCE OF THE MILITARY—TO MAKE THIS HAPPEN.

BEHIND THE WORDS

ALTHOUGH THE COURT'S DECISION IN *BROWN* WAS LIMITED TO PUBLIC SCHOOLS, THE POWERFUL RULING WAS AN IMPORTANT STEP THAT HELPED BREAK DOWN SEGREGATION IN OTHER PUBLIC AREAS.

THE POWER OF "NO"

Of all the stories that shaped the civil rights movement, one of the most powerful started with one woman's refusal to give up her seat on a bus. Rosa Parks lived in Montgomery, Alabama, where segregation laws required white and black riders to sit in separate sections of the bus.

On December 1, 1955, Parks took a seat at the front of the bus and later refused to give it to a white man. Her resistance led to her arrest and launched the Montgomery Bus **Boycott**. Rosa Parks described her brave act in simple terms: "People always say that I didn't give up my seat because I was tired, but that isn't true. . . . No, the only tired I was, was tired of giving in."

BEHIND THE WORDS

ROSA PARKS SAID, "EACH PERSON MUST LIVE THEIR LIFE AS A MODEL FOR OTHERS."

MONTGOMERY BUS BOYCOTT

FIRST TIME IN BALTIMORE!

HEAR!— **MRS. ROSA PARKS**

Whose arrest, because she refused to be segregated, led to the Bus Boycott in Montgomery, Alabama.

BALTIMORE BRANCH N.A.A.C.P.
KICK-OFF
MASS MEETING

SUNDAY, SEPTEMBER 23, 1956 - 3 P.M.
SHARP STREET METHODIST CHURCH
Dolphin and Etting Streets
—Music by Famous BALTIMORE CHORALE—
under direction of Gerald Burkes Wilson

RENEW YOUR MEMBERSHIP TODAY!
And Get One More!

Good Music   **Admission Free**
Mrs. Lillie M. Jackson, President   Dr. Charles Watts, Treasurer

ROSA PARKS PUT HERSELF AT GREAT RISK BY CHALLENGING AN UNFAIR LAW, BUT HER COURAGE HELPED CHANGE SOCIETY.

THE MOTHER OF THE CIVIL RIGHTS MOVEMENT

ROSA PARKS WAS BORN IN 1913 IN ALABAMA, WHERE RACIST PRACTICES HAD EXISTED LONG AFTER THE END OF SLAVERY. PARKS WORKED AS A **SEAMSTRESS** IN SEGREGATED MONTGOMERY, ALABAMA, AND BECAME THE SECRETARY OF MONTGOMERY'S NAACP CHAPTER IN 1943. HER FAMOUS REFUSAL TO SURRENDER HER SEAT SET IN MOTION A BUS BOYCOTT 381 DAYS LONG THAT INSPIRED OTHER PEACEFUL PROTESTS. FOR THESE REASONS, PARKS IS REMEMBERED BY MANY AS THE "MOTHER OF THE CIVIL RIGHTS MOVEMENT."

WRITING FROM JAIL

Out of the Montgomery Bus Boycott emerged the most famous leader of the civil rights movement: Dr. Martin Luther King Jr. At the time of the boycott, King was a 26-year-old minister who gained national attention for his nonviolent **tactics**—and his powerful words.

King had an exceptional talent for speaking and writing. He used it to inspire a nation of people to join him in the fight for civil rights. In 1963, King was arrested during a peaceful protest against Alabama's segregated lunch counters. From jail, King wrote a famous letter that explained his commitment to fighting discrimination through nonviolence. In the letter, King argued that all people, no matter where they live, have a role in the fight for equality, stating, "Injustice anywhere is a threat to justice everywhere."

BEHIND THE WORDS

IN HIS "LETTER FROM A BIRMINGHAM JAIL," KING SAID, "**OPPRESSED** PEOPLE CANNOT REMAIN OPPRESSED FOREVER. THE YEARNING FOR FREEDOM EVENTUALLY MANIFESTS [REVEALS] ITSELF."

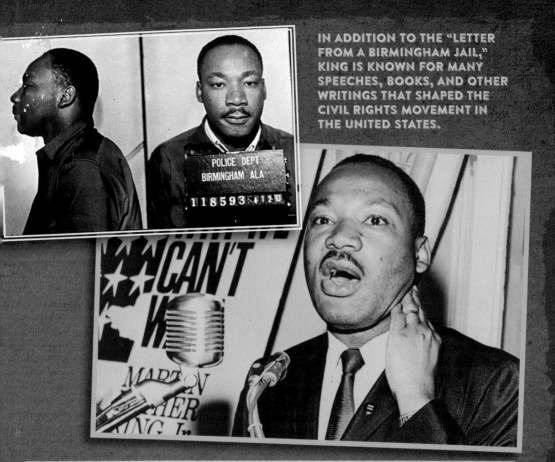

IN ADDITION TO THE "LETTER FROM A BIRMINGHAM JAIL," KING IS KNOWN FOR MANY SPEECHES, BOOKS, AND OTHER WRITINGS THAT SHAPED THE CIVIL RIGHTS MOVEMENT IN THE UNITED STATES.

A RIGHTEOUS RESPONSE

KING'S ARREST IN BIRMINGHAM MARKED THE THIRTEENTH TIME HE WAS JAILED FOR PROTESTING SEGREGATION, EVEN THOUGH THE PROTESTS WERE PEACEFUL AND NONVIOLENT. WHILE IN JAIL, KING SECRETLY RECEIVED A COPY OF THE LOCAL NEWSPAPER. IT CONTAINED A LETTER THAT CRITICIZED THE MOVEMENT. FROM JAIL, KING WROTE HIS RESPONSE IN PIECES, UNTIL IT WAS OVER 7,000 WORDS AND 21 PAGES LONG. HIS LETTER WAS PUBLISHED NATIONALLY AND CONTINUES TO INSPIRE PEOPLE AROUND THE WORLD TO ACT DURING TIMES OF INJUSTICE.

ENVISIONING THE DREAM

Of all Dr. Martin Luther King Jr.'s powerful speeches, there's perhaps none more memorable than the one he delivered on August 28, 1963, in Washington, DC. During the March on Washington for Jobs and Freedom, King stood before a crowd of about 250,000 people and shared his dream of America.

"I have a dream," King said, "that my four little children will one day live in a nation where they will not be judged by the color of their skin but by the content of their character." These now-famous words **captivated** the crowd and the nation. He asked that the American dream of freedom and equality be made possible for all citizens, regardless of race. He said, "Now is the time to make real the promises of **democracy**."

BEHIND THE WORDS

THE MARCH ON WASHINGTON PUT PRESSURE ON THE US GOVERNMENT TO PASS CIVIL RIGHTS LAWS. THE CIVIL RIGHTS ACT WAS PASSED IN 1964, AND THE VOTING RIGHTS ACT WAS PASSED IN 1965.

A SHORT BIOGRAPHY OF MLK

Martin Luther King Jr. was born in Atlanta, Georgia, in 1929. He's recognized as the most famous leader of the civil rights movement. His activism, which was defined by nonviolence and peaceful protests, helped bring an end to legal segregation in the United States. A Baptist minister, leader of the Southern Christian Leadership Conference (SCLC), and Nobel Peace Prize winner, King inspired millions to fight against inequality. He was killed in 1968, but his **LEGACY** has shaped America indefinitely.

KING REPEATED THE FAMOUS PHRASE "I HAVE A DREAM" EIGHT TIMES IN HIS SPEECH.

"BY ANY MEANS NECESSARY"

Malcolm X was a civil rights leader who, like Martin Luther King Jr., captivated the nation with his talent for speaking. However, unlike King, he doubted nonviolence could help African Americans achieve equality. Malcolm X believed that African Americans should fight back when they were treated unfairly, even if it meant turning to violence.

BEHIND THE WORDS

Toward the end of his life, Malcolm X said, "I know now that some white people are truly sincere, that some truly are capable of being brotherly toward a black man."

During a speech given in 1964, Malcolm X famously said, "We want freedom by any means necessary. We want justice by any means necessary. We want equality by any means necessary." By this, he meant that African Americans should demand equality however they could, rather than waiting for it to be given to them. It was statements like these that drew much attention to Malcolm X and set him apart in the civil rights movement.

MALCOLM X'S STIRRING WORDS ESTABLISHED HOW STRONGLY HE AND OTHER AFRICAN AMERICANS FELT ABOUT SECURING TRUE FREEDOM.

MALCOLM X AND THE BLACK NATIONALIST MOVEMENT

MALCOLM LITTLE WAS BORN IN NEBRASKA IN 1925. MALCOLM WAS ARRESTED FOR ROBBERY IN 1946. WHILE IN PRISON, HE BECAME A FOLLOWER OF THE NATION OF ISLAM. THIS GROUP BELIEVED IN BLACK NATIONALISM, A MOVEMENT THAT PROMOTED BLACK PRIDE AND THE IDEA THAT BLACK PEOPLE COULD BE FREE ONLY WHEN SEPARATE FROM WHITE SOCIETY. HOWEVER, MALCOLM X LATER CAME TO BELIEVE THAT BLACKS AND WHITES COULD LIVE TOGETHER PEACEFULLY. HE WAS KILLED IN 1965.

RIDE TO FREEDOM

In the segregated South, public transportation mirrored the unequal treatment of whites and blacks. In 1961, a group of brave activists, including students, set out to challenge the laws that forced black people to use separate areas of buses, bus stations, and restrooms when traveling between states.

The activists, both black and white, boarded a bus in Washington, DC, and set out for the Deep South. The Freedom Riders, as they were called, didn't know what lay ahead of them, but they knew their lives were at risk. They pressed on anyway, expecting the worst. James Farmer, organizer of the Freedom Rides, said, "When we began the ride, I think all of us were prepared for as much violence as could be thrown at us. We were prepared for the possibility of death."

FREEDOM RIDERS

A RISKY ROAD TO FREEDOM

THE FREEDOM RIDERS CHALLENGED SEGREGATION ON PUBLIC TRANSPORTATION THROUGHOUT THE SOUTH. THE FIRST WAVE ARRIVED BY BUS INTO ANNISTON, ALABAMA, ON MAY 14, 1961. A CROWD OF ANGRY PEOPLE ATTACKED THE BUS AND THE RIDERS, AND MANY OF THE RIDERS WERE HURT. COMMITTED TO THEIR PRINCIPLES OF NONVIOLENCE, THE FREEDOM RIDERS DIDN'T FIGHT BACK. THEIR COURAGE IN THE FACE OF HATRED EARNED THEM SUPPORT FOR THEIR CAUSE ACROSS THE COUNTRY.

JAMES FARMER WAS A FAMOUS CIVIL RIGHTS LEADER WHO FOUNDED THE CONGRESS OF RACIAL EQUALITY (CORE) AND ORGANIZED THE FREEDOM RIDES.

JAMES FARMER

BEHIND THE WORDS

JIM PECK, ONE OF THE WHITE FREEDOM RIDERS, RECEIVED 50 STITCHES AFTER BEING ATTACKED. YET HE SAID, "I THINK IT IS PARTICULARLY IMPORTANT AT THIS TIME WHEN IT HAS BECOME NATIONAL NEWS THAT WE CONTINUE AND SHOW THAT NONVIOLENCE CAN PREVAIL OVER VIOLENCE."

AN IMPASSIONED SPEAKER

One of the most passionate voices of the civil rights movement belonged to Fannie Lou Hamer. Hamer led a voting rights movement and championed economic opportunities for African Americans. She was known for her deeply honest speeches, which addressed issues head on. "Is this America," Hamer said, "the land of the free and the home of the brave, where . . . our lives be threatened daily, because we want to live as decent human beings?"

Hamer's statement was part of a speech before the Democratic National Convention in 1964, where she was running for Congress. In her speech, she described the racial prejudice she experienced as a black woman in the United States. She effectively showed how the American dream was little more than a broken promise for many Americans.

SECURING THE RIGHT TO VOTE

Fannie Lou Hamer was born in Mississippi in 1917. Throughout her life, she experienced discrimination that prompted her to become a leader of the civil rights activism that took place in Mississippi in the 1960s. Hamer joined the Student Nonviolent Coordinating Committee as a community organizer, helped found the Mississippi Freedom Democratic Party, and ran for Congress. Throughout her life, she focused on securing voting rights for African American citizens.

FANNIE LOU HAMER DELIVERED HER SPEECHES WITH A PASSION THAT MADE OTHERS PAY ATTENTION. OF HER HARD LIFE, SHE SAID, "ALL MY LIFE I'VE BEEN SICK AND TIRED. NOW I'M SICK AND TIRED OF BEING SICK AND TIRED."

BEHIND THE WORDS

HAMER'S 1964 SPEECH WAS SET TO AIR ON NATIONAL TELEVISION BUT WAS INTERRUPTED BY AN UNPLANNED TV APPEARANCE BY THEN-PRESIDENT LYNDON B. JOHNSON. THE PRESS ENDED UP PUBLISHING HER SPEECH, HOWEVER.

A STUDENT STANDS UP

The civil rights movement gained energy thanks to the efforts of famous leaders such as Martin Luther King Jr. But everyday citizens contributed, too. Students especially came together to protest unfair treatment of black citizens.

Diane Nash was a college student in the 1960s. A founder of the Student Nonviolent Coordinating Committee (SNCC), Nash

BEHIND THE WORDS

DIANE NASH SAID, "A LOT OF PEOPLE SAY, 'OH, YOU'RE SO BRAVE,' AND THINK I WASN'T AFRAID, BUT THAT IS NOT TRUE—I WAS REALLY, REALLY AFRAID."

organized peaceful protests and **sit-ins** at segregated lunch counters. In 1960, Nash led thousands of people in a silent march through the streets of Nashville, Tennessee. Upon arriving at City Hall, Nash bravely asked the mayor, "Do you feel that it's wrong to discriminate against a person, solely on the basis of his race or color?" The mayor agreed it was wrong. Nash demanded, "We ask you to stop segregation at the lunch counters."

SHORTLY AFTER DIANE NASH CONFRONTED NASHVILLE'S MAYOR, NASHVILLE BECAME THE FIRST SOUTHERN CITY TO DESEGREGATE LUNCH COUNTERS.

DIANE NASH

BORN TO LEAD

DIANE NASH'S CAREER AS A CIVIL RIGHTS ACTIVIST BEGAN AT A YOUNG AGE. SHE ATTENDED COLLEGE IN THE SEGREGATED SOUTH, WHERE HER EXPERIENCE WITH DISCRIMINATION SPARKED A DESIRE TO FIGHT FOR CHANGE. WHILE IN COLLEGE, NASH LEARNED ABOUT NONVIOLENT RESISTANCE. IN NASHVILLE, SHE PARTICIPATED IN LUNCH COUNTER SIT-INS AND PEACEFUL PROTESTS. FOLLOWING HER INVOLVEMENT IN THE SNCC, NASH BECAME A FREEDOM RIDER AND LED THE SELMA RIGHT-TO-VOTE MOVEMENT OF 1963.

THE CIVIL RIGHTS ACT
OF 1964

Slavery ended in 1865 with the passage of the Thirteenth Amendment. While the Fourteenth and Fifteenth Amendments guaranteed African Americans civil rights under the law, these laws weren't enforced. Racism went unchecked.

Leaders, activists, and everyday citizens devoted their lives to ending segregation. Finally, in 1964, their efforts paid off. On July 2, the Civil Rights Act became law. This act prohibits, or bans, discrimination in public facilities, schools, and hiring practices at places that receive federal funds. It reads, "All persons shall be entitled to the full and equal enjoyment of . . . public accommodation [the use of public places] . . . without discrimination or segregation on the ground of race, color, religion, or national origin." This law helped shape a new America.

PRESIDENT JOHNSON SIGNING THE CIVIL RIGHTS ACT

THE VOTING RIGHTS ACT

EVEN THOUGH AFRICAN AMERICANS HAD THE RIGHT TO VOTE, DISCRIMINATORY VOTING PRACTICES KEPT THEM FROM EXERCISING THIS RIGHT. THESE PRACTICES INCLUDED POLL TAXES, **LITERACY** TESTS, AND THE THREAT OF VIOLENCE WHEN ATTEMPTING TO REGISTER OR VOTE ON ELECTION DAYS. THE AFRICAN AMERICAN COMMUNITY WAS ROBBED OF POLITICAL POWER, WHICH KEPT THEM OPPRESSED. IN 1965, THE VOTING RIGHTS ACT OUTLAWED THESE PRACTICES. IT WAS ANOTHER MAJOR MOMENT IN THE CIVIL RIGHTS MOVEMENT.

LAWS OF THE CIVIL RIGHTS MOVEMENT

CIVIL RIGHTS ACT OF 1964	VOTING RIGHTS ACT OF 1965
IMPORTANCE: MADE IT ILLEGAL TO DISCRIMINATE ON THE BASIS OF RACE	IMPORTANCE: MADE DISCRIMINATORY VOTING PRACTICES ILLEGAL
IMPACT: PROTECTED AND ENFORCED AFRICAN AMERICANS' CIVIL RIGHTS	IMPACT: GUARANTEED AND PROTECTED AFRICAN AMERICANS' RIGHT TO VOTE

THE CIVIL RIGHTS MOVEMENT BROUGHT ABOUT TWO LAWS IN THE 1960S THAT CHANGED THE UNITED STATES.

BEHIND THE WORDS

THE VOTING RIGHTS ACT OF 1965 STATED: "NO VOTING QUALIFICATION . . . SHALL BE IMPOSED OR APPLIED BY ANY STATE OR POLITICAL SUBDIVISION TO DENY OR ABRIDGE [RESTRICT] THE RIGHT OF ANY CITIZEN OF THE UNITED STATES TO VOTE ON ACCOUNT OF RACE OR COLOR."

"UNBOUGHT AND UNBOSSED"

The civil rights movement paved the way for people to occupy spaces that, before, never seemed possible. In American politics, most leaders have been white men. In the 1960s, Shirley Chisholm entered the political arena, and her bold personality set her apart. "I want to be remembered as a woman . . . who dared to be a **catalyst** of change," she said.

Chisholm was the first African American congresswoman. During the 1968 congressional race, Chisholm campaigned against civil rights leader James Farmer. Her commitment to racial and gender equality helped her win a seat in Congress, a position she held until 1983. In 1972, Chisholm campaigned for the Democratic Party's presidential nomination. Though she didn't win it, "Fighting Shirley" left a lasting impression and inspired other black women to pursue politics.

BEHIND THE WORDS

SHIRLEY CHISHOLM'S CAMPAIGN MOTTO WAS "UNBOUGHT AND UNBOSSED," WHICH SPOKE TO HER HONEST VALUES AND STRONG PERSONALITY.

26

LEADING WOMEN

Like Shirley Chisholm, many female leaders played an important role in the civil rights era. Ella Baker helped organize the Student Nonviolent Coordinating Committee and convinced Martin Luther King Jr. to support it. Dorothy Height, the "godmother of the civil rights movement," helped organize the March on Washington and worked for women's rights. Angela Davis's activism brought attention to many social justice causes. Whether demanding race equality, gender equality, or both, these women fought for a better society.

DOROTHY HEIGHT

SHIRLEY CHISHOLM

SHIRLEY CHISHOLM WAS KNOWN FOR BEING OUTSPOKEN, SOMETHING SHE TOOK PRIDE IN. ABOUT HER POSITION IN CONGRESS, SHE ONCE SAID, "I HAVE NO INTENTION OF JUST SITTING QUIETLY AND OBSERVING."

THE LEGACY
LIVES ON

While the civil rights movement never came to an official end, it was never as united after Martin Luther King Jr.'s death in 1968. Yet, racism has persisted in many parts of life even today. Many activist groups continue to fight discrimination. Black Lives Matter is one such organization. Formed in 2013, this global network works to stop racist violence against African Americans as well as to tackle other serious issues. "We work vigorously for freedom and justice for Black people and, by extension, all people," the organization's website states.

Black Lives Matter is one of many activist groups that reflect the spirit of civil rights groups before them. Today, the words of the civil rights movement live on, leaving a legacy that continues to inspire people all over the world.

BEHIND THE WORDS

TODAY'S CIVIL RIGHTS ACTIVISTS USE **SOCIAL MEDIA** TO SPREAD IMPORTANT MESSAGES.

ACTIVISM IN THE 21ST CENTURY

Activism will be around as long as inequalities exist, and today, people are more connected than ever to national and global movements. Social activism is action taken to produce social change, such as improving racial equality and fighting for LGBTQ+ rights. Social activists are passionate about everything from improving conditions for the poor to protecting the planet, and everything in between. No matter the cause, social activists are united by one thing: They're fighting for something they believe in.

MAJOR MOMENTS OF THE CIVIL RIGHTS MOVEMENT OF THE 1950s AND 1960s

1961: THE FREEDOM RIDERS BEGIN TO CHALLENGE SEGREGATIONIST TRANSPORTATION LAWS.

1963: MARTIN LUTHER KING JR. WRITES HIS "LETTER FROM A BIRMINGHAM JAIL."
KING SPEAKS DURING THE MARCH ON WASHINGTON FOR JOBS AND FREEDOM.

1964: MALCOLM X FAMOUSLY SAYS, "WE WANT FREEDOM BY ANY MEANS NECESSARY."
THE CIVIL RIGHTS ACT IS PASSED.
FANNIE LOU HAMER SPEAKS BEFORE THE DEMOCRATIC NATIONAL CONVENTION ABOUT PREJUDICE AGAINST BLACK WOMEN.

1965: MALCOLM X IS KILLED.
THE VOTING RIGHTS ACT IS PASSED.

1968: MARTIN LUTHER KING JR. IS KILLED.
SHIRLEY CHISHOLM BECOMES THE FIRST AFRICAN AMERICAN CONGRESSWOMAN.

GLOSSARY

activist: one who acts strongly in support of or against an issue or cause

boycott: the act of refusing to have dealings with a person or business in order to force change

captivate: to attract and hold attention

catalyst: a person or event that quickly causes change or action

democracy: the free and equal right of every person to participate in a government

inherently: having to do with the basic nature of someone or something

legacy: something that is passed down from someone

literacy: the ability to read and write

oppress: to use power unjustly over another. Also, treating people in a cruel or unfair way.

prejudice: an unfair feeling of dislike for a group because of race, sex, religion, or other beliefs

seamstress: a woman who sews as a job

sit-in: a protest in which people stay in a place until they are given what they demand

social media: forms of electronic communication through which people create online communities to share information, ideas, and messages

tactic: a method for accomplishing a goal

FOR MORE INFORMATION

BOOKS

Blohm, Craig E. *The Civil Rights Movement*. San Diego, CA: ReferencePoint Press, 2019.

Randolph, Joanne, ed. *African American Politicians & Civil Rights Activists*. New York, NY: Enslow Publishing, 2018.

Terp, Gail. *Nonviolent Resistance in the Civil Rights Movement*. Minneapolis, MN: Core Library, 2016.

WEBSITES

10 Facts About Martin Luther King
www.natgeokids.com/za/discover/history/general-history/martin-luther-king-facts/
Learn 10 facts about Martin Luther King Jr. and read about his legacy.

Civil Rights Act (1964)
www.ourdocuments.gov/doc.php?flash=false&doc=97
Visit the National Archives website to learn more about the Civil Rights Act and view primary source images.

Publisher's note to educators and parents: Our editors have carefully reviewed these websites to ensure that they are suitable for students. Many websites change frequently, however, and we cannot guarantee that a site's future contents will continue to meet our high standards of quality and educational value. Be advised that students should be closely supervised whenever they access the internet.

INDEX